A TALE OF THREE WISHES

ISAAC BASHEVIS SINGER
A Tale of Three Wishes

PICTURES BY IRENE LIEBLICH

Farrar · Straus · Giroux · New York

A TALE OF THREE WISHES

Frampol. This was the name of the town. It had all the things that a town should have: a synagogue, a study house, a poorhouse, a rabbi, and a few hundred inhabitants. Each Thursday was market day in Frampol, when the peasants came from the hamlets to sell grain, potatoes, chickens, calves, honey, and to buy salt, kerosene, shoes, boots, and whatever else a peasant may need.

There were in Frampol three children who often played together: Shlomah, or Solomon, seven years old; his sister, Esther, six years old; and their friend Moshe, who was about Shlomah's age.

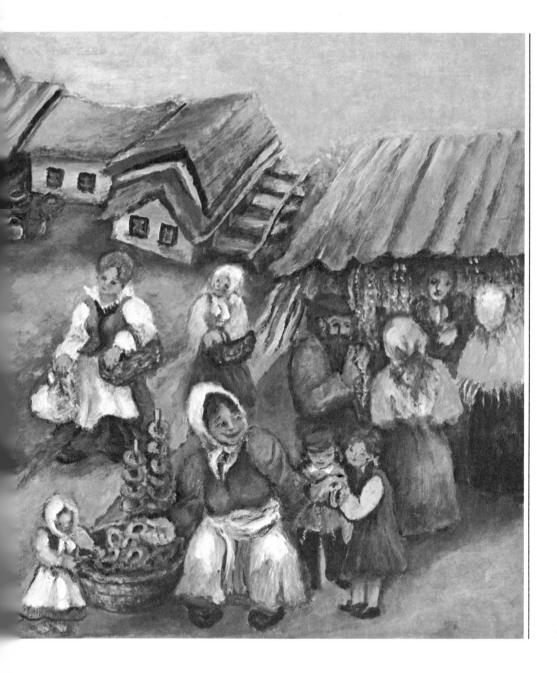

Shlomah and Moshe went to the same cheder and someone there told them that on Hoshanah Rabbah, which is the last day of the Feast of Tabernacles, the sky opens late at night. Those who see it happen have a minute's time to make a wish, and whatever they wish will come true.

Shlomah, Moshe, and Esther spoke of this often. Shlomah said that he would wish to be as wise and rich as King Solomon, his namesake. Moshe's wish was to be as learned in religion as was the famous Rabbi Moshe Maimonides. Esther desired to be as beautiful as Queen Esther. After long discussions, the three children decided to wait until Hoshanah Rabbah, to stay awake the whole night together and, when the sky opened, to utter their wishes.

Children must go to bed early, but the three stayed awake until their parents fell asleep. Then they sneaked out of the house and met in the synagogue yard to wait for the miraculous event.

12

It was quite an adventure. The night was moonless and cool. The children had heard that demons lurk outside, ready to attack those who dare to go out on a dark night. There was also talk of corpses who after midnight pray in the synagogue and read from the Holy Scroll. If someone passed by the synagogue at such a late hour, he might be called up to the reading table, a most frightening event. But Shlomah and Moshe had put on fringed garments, and Esther had dressed in two aprons, one in the front and one in the back, all meant to ward off the evil powers. Just the same, the children were afraid. An owl was hooting. Esther had been told that bats flew around at night and that if one of them got entangled in a girl's hair she would die within the year. Esther had covered her hair tightly with a kerchief.

An hour passed, two hours, three, and still the sky did not open. The children became tired and even hungry. Suddenly there was lightning and the sky opened. The children saw angels, seraphim, cherubim, fiery chariots, as well as the ladder which Jacob saw in his dream, with winged angels going up and down, just as it is written in the Bible. It all happened so quickly that the children forgot their wishes.

Esther spoke up first, "I'm hungry. I wish I had a blintz."

At once, a blintz appeared before the children's eyes.

When Shlomah saw that his sister had wasted her wish on such a petty thing as a blintz, he became enraged and cried out, "You silly girl, I wish you were a blintz yourself."

In an instant, Esther became a blintz. Only her face looked out from the dough, pale and frightened.

Moshe had loved Esther for as long as he could remember. When he saw that his beloved Esther had turned into a blintz, he fell into terrible despair. There was no time to lose. The minute was almost over, and he exclaimed, "I wish her to be as she was."

And so it happened.

Immediately the sky closed again.

When the children realized how foolishly they had squandered their wishes, they began to cry. The night had become pitch black and they could not find their way back home. They seemed to be lost in some strange place. There were no mountains in Frampol; still, the children were climbing up a mountain. They tried to walk down again, but their feet kept climbing by themselves. Then there appeared an old man with a white beard. In one hand he held a stick, in the other a lantern with a candle inside. His robe was girded with a white sash. A strong wind was blowing, but the candle did not flicker.

The old man asked, "Where are you going? And why are you crying?"

Shlomah told him the truth, how they stayed awake all night and how they wasted their wishes.

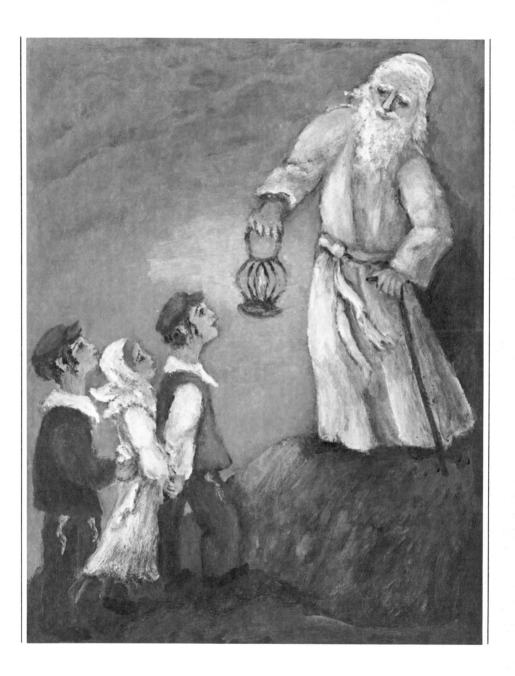

The old man shook his head. "No good wish is ever wasted."

"Perhaps the demons confused us and made us forget our wishes," Moshe suggested.

"No demons have any power in the holy night of Hosha-nah Rabbah," the old man said.

"So why did the sky play such a trick on us?" Esther asked.

"Heaven does not play tricks," the old man answered. "You were the ones who tried to play tricks on heaven. No one can become wise without experience, no one can become a scholar without studying. As for you, little girl, you are pretty already, but beauty of the body must be paired with beauty of the soul. No young child can possess the love and the devotion of a queen who was ready to sacrifice her life for her people. Because you three wished too much, you received nothing."

"What shall we do now?" the children asked.

"Go home and try to deserve by effort what you wanted to get too easily."

"Who are you?" the children asked, and the old man replied, "On high, they call me The Watcher in the Night."

As soon as he said these words, the children found themselves back in the synagogue yard. They were so weary that the moment they came home and put their heads on their pillows, they fell asleep. They never told anybody what had happened to them. It remained their secret.

Years passed. Shlomah had become more and more eager for knowledge. He showed so much talent and studied so many books of history, trade, and finance that he became the adviser of the King of Poland. They called him the King without a Crown, and King Solomon of Poland. He married the daughter of an important man and became famous for his wisdom and charity.

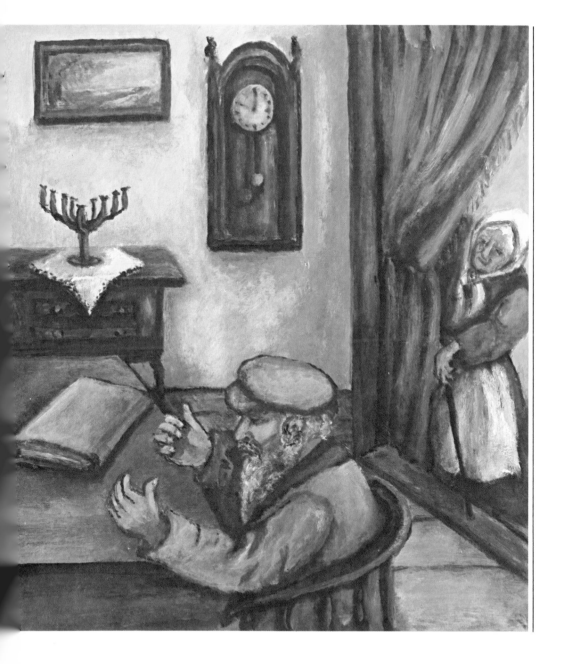

Moshe had always been deeply interested in religion. He knew the Bible and the Talmud almost by heart. He wrote many religious books and he became known as The Maimonides of Our Time.

Esther grew up to be not only beautiful but a learned and highly virtuous young lady. Many young men from rich houses sent matchmakers to her parents to ask for her hand in marriage, but Esther loved only Moshe, as he loved only her.

When the old rabbi of Frampol died, Moshe was made rabbi of the town. A rabbi must have a wife, and Rabbi Moshe married his Esther.

All the people of Frampol attended the wedding. The bride's brother, Shlomah, came to his sister's wedding in a carriage drawn by six horses, with grooms riding in front and on the back of the carriage. There was music and dancing, and the young couple received many gifts. Late at

night, the bridegroom was called to dance with the bride, and so were all the guests, the bride holding one edge of the handkerchief and her partner the other, according to custom. When someone asked if everyone had danced with the bride, the wedding jester said: "Yes, except for the night watchman." As he uttered these words, an old man emerged from nowhere with a stick in one hand, a lantern in the other hand, his loins girded with a white sash. The bride, her brother, and the bridegroom recognized the old man, but they kept silent. He approached the bride, placed the lantern and the stick on a bench nearby, and began to dance with her, all the people staring in amazement and awe. No one had ever seen this old man before. The band stopped playing. It became so quiet that one could hear the sputtering of the candles and the chirping of the grasshoppers outside. Then the old man lifted up his lantern and gave it to Rabbi Moshe, saying, "Let this light show you the way in the Torah." He offered the stick to Shlomah with the words: "Let this stick protect you from all your enemies." To Esther, who was holding the white sash, he said: "Let this sash bind you to your people and their needs forever."

After saying these words, the old man vanished.

In the years following, it happened quite often that the Jews came to ask Esther to intercede for them before the rulers of the land. She would fasten the white sash around her waist, and she never failed to help her people. Everyone called her Queen Esther.

Whenever Rabbi Moshe had difficulties in understanding some fine point of the law, he opened the ark where the lantern stood with its eternal light, and things became clear to him. When Shlomah was in trouble, he would take hold of the stick and his foes became powerless.

All three lived to a ripe old age. Only before his death did

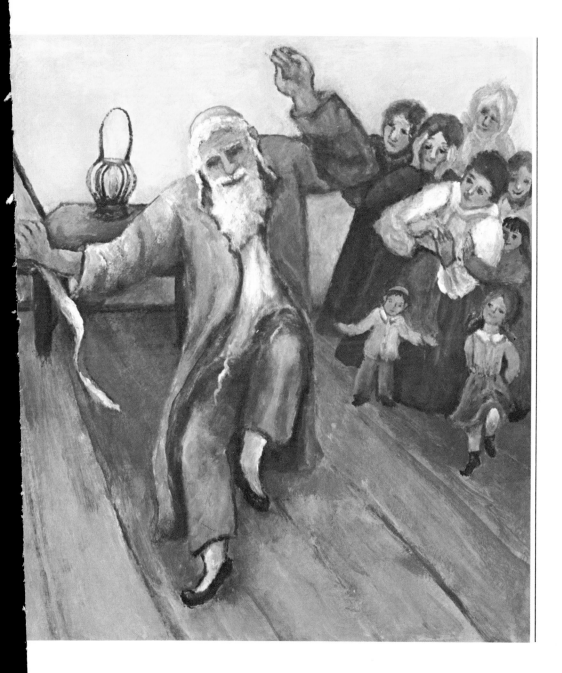

Rabbi Moshe reveal to the people of Frampol what had happened that night of Hoshanah Rabbah. The rabbi said, "For those who are willing to make an effort, great miracles and wonderful treasures are in store. For them the gates of heaven are always open."